LONG AGO, WHEN THE WORLD WAS JUST A BABY, A FAMILY OF GODS LIVED IN GREECE. THEY LIVED ON MOUNT OLYMPUS, ABOVE CLOUDS THAT LOOKED LIKE WHIPPED CREAM. THEY WERE ALL GODS OF ONE THING OR ANOTHER...

ME, ON OLYMPUS

LIKE ALL GODS IN THOSE DAYS, I WAS FULLY GROWN IN AN HOUR AND FIFTEEN MINUTES. I WAS GIVEN MY VERY OWN THRONE.

BUT SITTING ON A THRONE ALL DAY WASN'T MUCH FUN. IN FACT—IT WAS REALLY BORING!

NO WONDER EVERYONE WAS SO GRUMPY. I DECIDED TO CHEER THINGS UP...

EVERYONE FELT A NEW FEELING THAT MADE THEM LEAP, YELP, AND QUIVER!

IT'S A NEW FEELING I JUST INVENTED. I CALL IT PANIC, AFTER ME!
WHAT ABOUT ME? SHOULDN'T I GET A LITTLE CREDIT?
FROM THEN ON I USED PANIC WHENEVER MY NAPS WERE DISTURBED. SOMETIMES I USED IT TO HELP FRIENDS AGAINST ENEMIES AND SOMETIMES I USED IT JUST FOR FUN: TO SCARE THE WITS OUT OF EVERYONE. SOONER OR LATER, EVERYBODY GOT A TASTE OF PANIC.

THE MOON WAS SO ANGRY I'D TRIED TO FOOL HER, SHE HID FOR WEEKS IN THE EARTH'S SHADOW— IT WAS THE FIRST ECLIPSE. I SWORE I WOULD NEVER FALL IN LOVE AGAIN. (BUT I WOULD.)

THE MONSTER TYPHON

One misty weekend morning while I slept in Arcadia and the other gods dozed on Olympus, the monster Typhon decided to make trouble. Her body was a coiled spring. Her eight arms had viper fingers. Her jackass ears knocked stars out of the sky.

But the worst thing about her was her voice. She could sound like a bellowing bull or a roaring lion or a litter of hungry puppies, a siamese cat, a flock of Canada geese, or a hurricane. She bounced quietly up Mount Olympus and made all her noises at once.

I SHOUTED MY LOUDEST, MOST HORRIBLE SHOUTS. TYPHON YELPED, LEAPT, AND QUIVERED IN **PANIC**. THAT GAVE HERMES LOTS OF TIME TO GRAB ZEUS'S SINEWS.

WAAAKE UP!!!

I THINK I GOT HER ATTENTION!

WHAT WAS THAT?

He went home to bed and was still giggling in his sleep.

But that night his words sprouted from the ground.
By morning they had grown into leaves of grass. When the breeze blew, the grass rustled, sighed, and whispered, "Midas has jackass ears! Midas has jackass ears!" for all the world to hear.

JACKASS EARS MIDAS HAS JACKASS EARS JACKASS EA
MIDAS HAS JACKASS
HA
JACKASS EA
MIDAS HAS
HAS
MIDAS HAS JACKASS EARS MIDAS HAS JACKASS EARS
MIDAS HAS JACKASS EARS MIDAS HAS JACKASS EARS
JACKASS EARS MIDAS HAS JACKASS EARS
MIDAS HAS JACKASS EARS MIDA
JACKASS EARS MIDAS HAS JACKASS EARS MIDA
MIDAS HAS JACKASS EARS MIDAS HA
EARS MIDAS HAS JACKASS EARS MIDAS HA
EARS MIDAS HAS JACKASS EARS
EARS MIDAS HAS JACKASS EARS MIDAS HAS JACKASS

MIDAS HAS JACKASS EAR
MIDAS HAS JACKASS EAR
MIDAS HAS JACKASS EAR
MIDAS HAS JACKASS EARS
MIDAS HAS JACKASS EARS MIDAS HAS JACKASS EARS
MIDAS HAS JACKASS EARS MIDAS HAS JACKASS

Apollo and heard up on Olympus and roared with laughter. Then we played a duet.
Poor Midas. Later Apollo took pity and gave his original ears back.

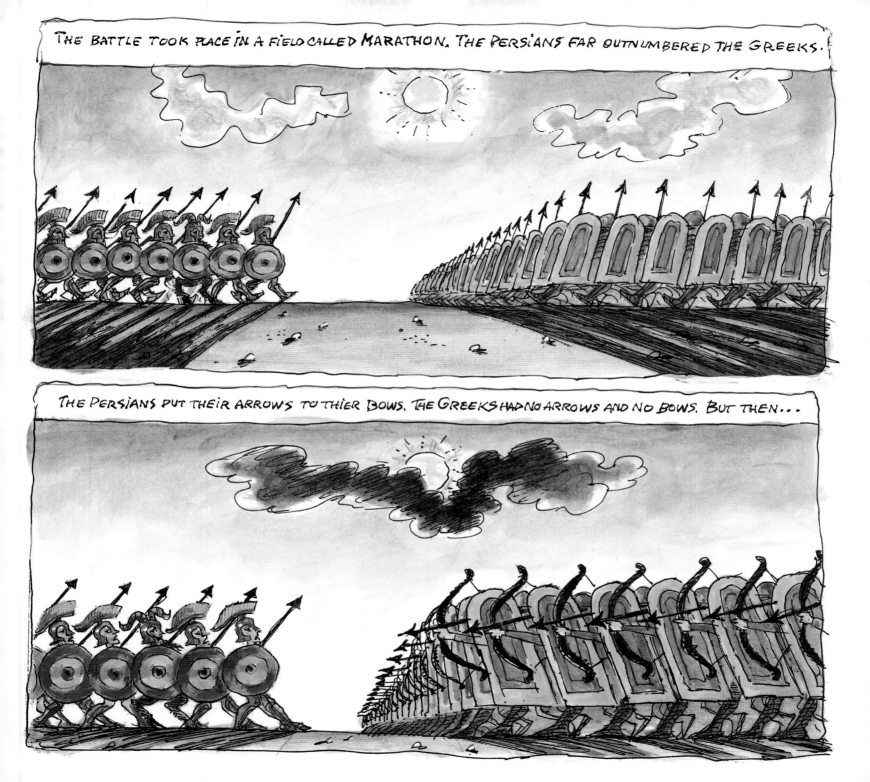

THE PERSIANS PANICKED AND THE BATTLE WAS OVER. PHIDIPPIDES RAN THE TWENTY-SEVEN MILES BACK TO ATHENS WITH THE GOOD NEWS. THAT'S WHY, TO THIS DAY, A RACE OF THAT LENGTH IS CALLED A MARATHON. ME? I WENT BACK TO MY ROCKY PEAKS AND PIPED FOR EAGLES.

ME DEAD?

THE CENTURIES ROLLED BY LIKE A PARADE OF CLOUDS ALONG THE HORIZON. PEOPLE SAILED NEW SEAS, FOUGHT NEW WARS, AND WORSHIPPED NEW GODS. THE WORLD GREW BIGGER AND GREECE LOOKED SMALLER. ONE STORMY NIGHT, A SAILOR NAMED THAMMUZ HEARD WAILING IN THE WIND AND THUNDER.

THAMMUZ! THE GREAT GOD **PAN** IS DEAD! THE GREAT WISE, WITTY, WILD, WONDERFUL, BRAVE, HANDSOME GOD **PAN** IS DEAD!

THE TRUTH IS, IT WAS ME WHO ANNOUNCED MY DEATH. MY FAMILY AND I WERE TIRED OF BEING GODS. TOO MUCH RESPONSIBILITY. WE ALL DECIDED TO RETIRE AND HAVE MORE FUN.

ALL THE OTHERS DISGUISED THEMSELVES AND ARE LIVING SOMEWHERE IN GREECE — OR IS IT CANADA? YOU CAN'T TELL THEM FROM ANY OTHER FAMILY.

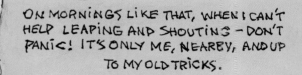

ON MORNINGS LIKE THAT, WHEN I CAN'T HELP LEAPING AND SHOUTING — DON'T PANIC! IT'S ONLY ME, NEARBY, AND UP TO MY OLD TRICKS.

AUTHOR'S NOTE

Most of the retellings of the Greek myths I've seen take the stories and characters quite seriously. Or they treat the gods and heroes as superheroes, telling us how great, grand, and powerful they were. But from my reading of Ovid, Hesiod, Robert Graves, and the Homeric Hymns, the Olympians could also be bad-tempered, silly, jealous, vengeful, and even stupid—more like characters in a family sitcom. They're interesting because they're so human, and so entertaining.

The silliest of them was Pan, the god of noise and confusion; the one who delighted all the other gods. A perfect deity for kids, because, though fully grown, at heart he's one of them. The ancient Greeks sang hymns to Pan. "All hail Pan, goat-footed, two-horned lover of noise and chaos!" They made him offerings of flowers and honey, but they also liked to gossip about him and his relatives. To me, that's what these myths are: gossip about the gods.

From all the sources I could find, I collected the tales in which Pan plays a part, and, using the actual myths, retell most of them here—maybe embellished just a bit. Here's a list of my main sources; see for yourself how wacky these Olympians were!

—Mordicai Gerstein

BIBLIOGRAPHY

Graves, Robert. *The Greek Myths*. Baltimore: Penguin, 1957.

Ovid. *Metamorphoses*. Trans. Rolfe Humphries. Bloomington: Indiana University Press, 1955.

Sargent, Thelma (trans.). *The Homeric Hymns: A Verse Translation*. New York: Norton, 1975.

Wender, Dorothea (ed.). *Hesiod and Theognis*. Middlesex: Penguin Classics, 1979.

For my delightful son, Aram Amadeus, with all my love

Text and Illustrations copyright © 2016 by Mordicai Gerstein
Published by Roaring Brook Press
Roaring Brook Press is a division of Holtzbrinck Publishing Holdings Limited Partnership
175 Fifth Avenue, New York, New York 10010
mackids.com

Library of Congress Cataloging-in-Publication Data
Gerstein, Mordicai, author, illustrator.
    I am Pan / written and illustrated by Mordicai Gerstein.
        pages cm
    Summary: "A picture book about the Greek god of the wild, shepherds,
music, hunting and misrule, Pan."— Provided by publisher.
    Audience: Ages 5–9.
    ISBN 978-1-62672-035-0 (hardcover)
    1. Pan (Greek deity)—Juvenile literature.   2. Gods, Greek—Juvenile
literature.   I. Title.
    BL820.P2G46 2016
    292.2'113—dc23
                                                        2014033005

Our books may be purchased in bulk for promotional, educational, or business use.
Please contact your local bookseller or the Macmillan Corporate and Premium Sales Department
at (800) 221-7945 ext. 5442 or by e-mail at MacmillanSpecialMarkets@macmillan.com.

First edition 2016
Book design by Andrew Arnold
Printed in China by RR Donnelley Asia Printing Solutions Ltd.,
Dongguan City, Guangdong Province
1   3   5   7   9   10   8   6   4   2   1